Elena
Va

ca

rescu, Carmen Sylva, Alma Strettell

The Bard of the Dimbovitza

Rovmanian folk-songs collected from the peasants

Elena
Va

ca

rescu, Carmen Sylva, Alma Strettell

The Bard of the Dimbovitza
Rovmanian folk-songs collected from the peasants

ISBN/EAN: 9783337331689

Printed in Europe, USA, Canada, Australia, Japan

Cover: Foto ©Andreas Hilbeck / pixelio.de

More available books at **www.hansebooks.com**

THE BARD OF THE DIMBOVITZA & &

ROVMANIAN FOLK-SONGS
SECOND SERIES

COLLECTED FROM THE PEASANTS BY

HÉLÈNE VACARESCO ⌐Elena Vӑcӑrescӑ⌐

TRANSLATED BY

CARMEN SYLVA

AND

ALMA STRETTELL

M.DCC · C.XCIV

OSGOOD, McILVAINE & CO.
45, ALBEMARLE STREET
LONDON, W.

INTRODUCTION.

THE appreciative reception given by the English public
to the first volume of translations made from Mdlle.
Vacaresco's remarkable collection of Roumanian Folk-
Songs, has encouraged the translators to put forth another
series of poems rendered into English from the same source,
in the hope that they may be received with equal favour.

Those who are familiar with the first volume of the
"Bard of the Dimbovitza," will remember that the songs
were collected in this one district of Roumania, to which
they are peculiar, and that Mdlle. Vacaresco laboured for
several years, with great perseverance and skill, to note
them down from the lips of the peasantry.

Such readers will not need to be told again of the
"Heiduck," the traditional hero and warrior of Roumanian
legend, the central figure of the romantic dreams of every
peasant maiden—or of the luteplayer, on whose lips
most of these songs may be heard, as he wanders from door
to door, accompanying himself on the lute or "cobza,"
from which his name is derived.

They will also be familiar with the peculiar construction

of these poems, which are generally unrhymed, and "depend more for rhythm on the cadence of each phrase, than on any definite poetical form." It would be both difficult and unsatisfactory to give examples of the monotonous chants to which they are usually sung, as on the peasants' lips they are unaccompanied by any instrument, the Cobzar only singing to his lute.

In the present selection will be found one poem which is sung by the youths, the maidens, and the Cobzar, alternately, during the "Hora," or national dance, and while the dancers move slowly round and round in a circle.

Another poem, " The Incantation," bears witness to the belief in witches and spells still existing in Roumania ; and Mdlle. Vacaresco herself was present at just such a scene as the song calls up before us, when the witch began her "spells" by waving a bough of hazel-wood over the dead ashes on her hearth.

The poem called " Mad " has a pathetic interest from the fact that it is not an imaginary composition, but was actually overheard, and noted down, from the lips of a woman who had gone distraught upon the loss of her lover. This poor creature could never be got to stay in her cottage, but haunted a wood near the Vacaresco house, where she would, of an evening, "light the fire " that she speaks of, and could be heard singing her song beside it.

A few explanatory notes have been added for those readers who are not familiar with the first volume of the series.

CONTENTS.

LUTEPLAYER'S SONGS.

B

LUTEPLAYER'S SONGS.

THE LUTEPLAYER'S AUTUMN SONG.

To-morrow the leaves will fall,
But I only think of the gold of the harvests to come ;
So glorious the splendour will be of those harvests to come,
That we never think again of the leaves that are falling.

WHEN she comes by
I go from hence, for then she must know that I love her ;
If she cross my path, I grow dumb, and beneath my fingers
I bid the cobza to hush, till the songs all ask me :
  "Why dost thou bid us keep silence ?"
  "Hush !" I make answer, "for now my love goeth
      by."
But when she abideth afar, oh then ! as the summer
Doth sing of the fleeting springtide, I sing of her.
I love her step in the dance, and its stir and rustle,
  For it bids her girdle dance, and the flowers in her
      hair.
When thou goest, O maiden, past the hut of thy Cobzar,
Let fall the flower from thy hair beside his door,

For then it will strike root before my threshold,
 And be to me a memory of thy soul.
The apple-tree felt light wings among its branches,
 And said: "How soft and light!"
 Soft is the hay, that lies on the plain, to the footfall,
Yet thou dost not sit thee down 'mid the new-mown
   hay.
When thou drawest water, O maiden! thou dost not suffer
The water to keep the image it hath of thee,
And yet thou hast told my heart to keep it for ever.
As I wander on, I sing, if thou be not near me;
I know full sure, the spell that would chain thee to me,
But I do not say the words, when thou goest by me,
For I love the stir and rustle of thy dancing
When it sets thy girdle gaily dancing too.
The gentle dreams of thy sleeping hours, I love them,
As I love the whirring of thy spindle fleet.
Refresh me with cool drink from the wooden pitcher,
For the weary wanderer's thirst is dear to thee;
And whoso doth quench such thirst is beloved of Heaven,
That blesses the springs and rivers, which be not sparing
 Nor from the wanderer cruelly turn away.
Beloved of Heaven, too, are the stars, that never
Withdraw themselves, nor hide their light from any,
Even from those who ne'er have looked on them.

I will pass away into Death, if thou let me die,
And never betray the place of my burial to thee;

Thou shalt ask the paths : " Which way doth lead to his
     gravestone ? "
And other men's graves shall answer thee aloud :
        " We are not his grave."
Then among the graves thou wilt wander with airy
     footfall,
For I ever loved the rustle and stir of thy dancing,
That bids thy girdle dance, and the flowers in thy hair.

To-morrow the leaves will fall,
But I only think of the gold of the harvests to come ;
So glorious the splendour will be of those harvests to come,
That we never think again of the leaves that are falling.

"ACCURSED."

The heavens lower, and the ravens fly.
Are ye forerunners of the snow, dark birds?
And shall we soon have snow upon our fields?

IT was not me he cursed, he cursed my house.
   And when I leave the house, my soul hath rest;
But when I enter in again, the curse
      Awaits me at my door.
   Would I might sleep beneath the open sky!
   But at the moonlight hour, One saith to me :
      "Go back into thy house."
Nor can I answer: "Nay, a curse is on it."
   It was not me he cursed,
He only cursed the bed whereon I sleep;
   Would I might lie upon the ground to sleep!
But at the hour of sleep, One saith to me :
      "Lie down upon thy bed."
It was not me he cursed, he only cursed
   The food that was to nourish me,
      The water that I drink.
   Would I might die of hunger!
But at the hour of hunger and of thirst,
   There crieth One aloud within me, saying:

"Eat then, and drink!"
It was not me he cursed;
He only cursed the paths I wander by;
  Would I might stay my steps!
  But at the hour of sunrise cometh One
And openeth wide my door and saith: "Go hence!"
  It was not me he cursed,
Only my chain, my girdle and my spindle;
  Would I need never touch them!
  But then One saith: "Take up
Thy girdle and thy spindle and thy chain."
  It was not me he cursed;
But only all I see and touch, and those
        To whom I draw me near.
And I would fain see nothing more, nor touch,
        Nor draw me near to any.
And to the graves I go, that I may die;
Then from the graves One riseth and saith: "Live!"

        The heavens lower, and the ravens fly.
        Are ye forerunners of the snow, dark birds?
        And will there soon be snow upon our fields?

THE ORPHAN.

One scarce can see the moonlight in the gloaming,
But when night falls, it lights up all the heavens.
The rivers, they are sisters, since they flow
Down from the self-same mountain.

Go not at night-time through the village;
The dogs sleep not—thou mightest, too, meet souls.—

But yet I bade my mother's soul to wait
Beside the well for me.
Into the well I shall look down to see her,
Yet shall not dare to gaze upon her face;
But she will take a long, long look at me,
To see my face, my girdle and my shift.
And then upon my girdle there will be
Many more pearls to-morrow, on my shift
More golden spangles.
Upon the house, too, she will look, and then
Sunshine will linger round the house to-morrow.
Upon my heart, too, she will look, and then
My heart will be at rest.
And I shall ask: "How is it in the grave?"
Then shall I see her image, in the well,
With finger on its lip.

And I shall ask her: "Dost thou yearn for me?"
Then shall I see her image in the well,
    Drying its eyes;
And in her girdle I shall see the flowers,
    Yea, all the flowers I cast upon her grave.
And nothing will she say to me, but I shall feel her glance.
Then she will make a sign to me, that I should give her
      drink;
    And in her name
I will bring drink to all the village huts.
And oh! how I shall grieve, because the well
Is all too deep for me to kiss her image.
I shall still seek her after she is gone,
Then shall I hear the stone that falls again
Upon her grave, as though it struck my heart.
For by the well I bade my mother's soul
    To wait for me.

One scarce can see the moonlight in the gloaming,
But when night falls, it lights up all the heavens.
The rivers, they are sisters, since they flow
    Down from the self-same mountain.

THE NECKLACE OF TEARS.

The Luteplayer sang before my cottage door;
I hearkened to his lay and said: "Sing on!"
But the Cobzar, he only knows one song.

The little maid was fain to make herself
      A necklace fine,
As silv'ry as the moonlight's silv'ry glance,
  Or as the river when the moonbeams shine.

And so she asked the river: "Speak, wilt thou
  Give me thy waves that in the moonlight dance?"—
And then she went and asked the moon: "Wilt thou
      Give me thy glance?"

"Not so," the moon replied, "because the night,
      My glance doth need."—
"Not so," the river answered her, "for I
  Must keep my waters for the thirsty mead."

The little maid was fain to make herself
      A necklace fine;
Then said the sons of men: "Come, take our tears
  To fashion this bright silver chain of thine."

Then each one gave her his most precious tears,
  And glad were they
To deck the maiden's throat ; and all the tears
  Thus whispered low together, and did say :

"Whence art thou, sister, from what heart dost come ?"
Then each one told the grief that did befall
Her parent heart, and each one thought herself
    Saddest of all.

So now the maiden had her necklace bright,
More silvery than yonder river's wave,
Or glance of moonlight, yet when she put on
    That necklace brave,   .

The tears all told her whence they came, and grew
So heavy, that beneath the burden sore,
The maiden died, and on her grave that chain
    Weighs evermore.

  The Luteplayer sang without my cottage door ;
  I hearkened to his lay and said : "Sing on !"
  But the Cobzar, he knows one only song.

420626

THE SOLDIER'S SONG.

The leaves all strove together in the forest,
  Because the wind passed through;
The leaves all strove together in the forest,
  And sore the forest grieved;
Yet in the forest strove the leaves together
  Because the wind passed through.

ERE I go to the wars, O mother mine,
  Take thou me by the hand,
And bless my weapon, and softly lay
  Thy finger on my brow,
And the sign of the cross thou shalt make thereon,
  Watch over me shall keep
    The while I sleep.
The ways shall be white that I travel by;
  The maidens shall come forth
And stand at their doors and give me smiles;
  And forth the sun shall come
From behind the clouds, and be all amazed
  When he sees how cheerful I can be,
    Cheerful as he.
For when he is dying, he hides him not;
  And when my hour is nigh,

I will shine, O mother, and glow with light
    Because I go forth to die.
The bird that gave me its plumes for my cap
    Will be glad of it by and by,
For one of those plumes shall be reddened with blood,
    Because I go forth to die.
And thy kiss, my bride, my little bride,
    That close on my mouth doth lie,
It will not be loth to rest on my lips,
    Because I go forth to die.
And the sign of the cross that thou mad'st o'er me,
    Will be glad I go forth to die.

When I am dead, little mother mine,
Then charge the heavens, the sun, the stars,
    To look yet on me in my death,
    So that they surely all may know
How brave a child, O mother! thou hast borne.
And go thou by my bride's low door
    What time she makes the old well shriek
        In drawing water up ;
Or when she calls the turtle-doves about her
        In going through the wood ;
    Then tell her of the soldier's death,
Speaking as of some other man
        Unto some other maid ;
But if my sweetheart drop her spindle, saying :
    " That was a hero ! "

There stood two men and they did point their fingers at
      that house,
And on his finger one had blood; the other's finger
      shook.
" How many kisses ? " asked the one, and then the other
      asked :
" How many tears ? " A maiden, too, stood there and
      watched the men,
And with the spindle in her hand, she pointed at the house.

A bridge across the river lies, and the river every spring
      Doth bear the bridge away.   ·

The spindle in the maiden's hand, it shook and trembled
      too. . . .
White was her shift—about her neck a crimson chain of
      blood.
" That was my house," she spake—once more : " That
      was my threshold-stone."
Then back she wended to her grave, and to her grave sank
      down.
And still the men did stand and point their fingers at that
      house.

Take whichsoever way thou wilt—the ways are all
      alike ;

AT THE HOUSE.

Take whichsoever way thou wilt, for the ways are all alike;
But do thou only come—I bade my threshold wait thy
coming.
From out my window one can see the graves—and on my life
The graves, too, keep a watch.

AND hast thou, sister, asked the wind from whence he
comes to-night,
That such strange things he tells?
Him whom I love, I never knew—yet I knew that if he
came
He would bring pain to me.

A bridge across the river lies, and the river every spring
Doth bear the bridge away.

Oh sister, hark! to-night the wind from far away doth
blow!
To-day he saw a house that stands with windows open
wide.
And lo! the house forsaken was, and black the threshold-
stone.

THE INCANTATION.

THOU little hazel-bough,
Thou that dost grow so near the river
That it is fain to kiss thee,
Thou that wilt never see the sun,
Because thou growest all too near the river,
I plucked thee when the sun knew nought thereof,
Upon my left breast I did bear thee hither,
And 'twixt my fingers took thee.

Fall on the ashes gently—do not stir them,
    For ashes love to slumber;
Hide close beneath them—and then go thy way,
    Thou little hazel-bough;
Then shall the tree from which thou camest forth
    Bear loveliest buds in April,
If thou wilt go, thither where I shall bid thee,
    Where my belovèd dwells.

He sleeps.   Now shalt thou ask him if he dream,
    And bid him dream of me.
Thou shalt become the sorrow of his heart,
    O little hazel-bough;

And tell him that the sorrow of his heart
    Dreams but of me ;
Thou shalt disturb his life with a desire.

Where is my sweetheart ?—speak, when will he come ?
    I have charged sleep to leave him ;
The water that he drinks, to bring before him
    In every drop mine image ;
The fragrance of his bread, to call my kiss
    To his remembrance.
His couch shall murmur all my songs to him,
The whiteness of my veil encompass him
    Even as the light ;
My step shall sound unceasing in his ears,
    And it shall seem to him
As though he saw me always coming toward him,
    Yet never reach the goal.
And when his house saith : " Hither come and rest,"
Then shall he answer : " Rest dwells not in thee ; "
And to the threshold's stone he thus shall speak :
    " Thou dreary stone ! "
And to the merry birds : " How sad ye are ! "
And to the sorrowing grave : " How glad art thou ! "
Nor ever shall he taste his bread's sweet savour
Without complaint, till he hath had my kiss.

    This shalt thou do, thou little hazel-bough,
    Thou that dost grow so near the river

That it is fain to kiss thee,
Thou that canst never see the sun
Because thou growest all too near the river.

"MY MOTHER WENT AWAY FROM ME.'

(GIPSY SONG.)

My mother went away from me—so wide and vast the plain;
My fire will soon be dying out, as stars at daybreak wane.
Art thou not coming back, O love, to feed the fire again?

BESIDE my fire the wand'rer sat him down,
    Since then it dieth out.
And with the wand'rer, too, my soul went hence.
Whither my soul went, now I ne'er can know,
Because he told not, whither went his steps.
The forest saw him pass, and said to me:
"I could not keep the wand'rer in my shade."
The river said: "Nor I upon my banks."

A Heiduck he was, I know, one of the race of the
    Heiducks,
Who are never weary of fighting, whom the sun doth love
    to see;
And whom the dreams of maidens do also love to see!
"What shall I bring thee back from the wars?" he asked
    me—
"Wilt thou the finest veil—wilt thou the slend'rest
    spindle?

A girdle all full of pearls, or a silver necklet heavy
To lie on thy little heart, and burden it with its weight ?
A bracelet wilt thou have, that shall ring upon thine arm ?
Or wilt thou have my heart, wherein thy heart hath
        nested ?
What shall I bring ? " Then I said : " I would rather
        have blood than all ;
That will redden my girdle so white with the reddest of
        pearls,
That will weigh down my necklet of silver, and make my
        bracelet
    Ring merrily on mine arm.
I will lay it, too, on the heart whereon my heart hath
        nested.
And shall not then both hearts grow warm thereby ? "
        I said ;
    —" I would rather have blood than all ! "

My mother went away from me—so wide and vast the plain ;
My fire will soon be dying out, as stars at daybreak wane.
Art thou not coming back, O love, to feed the fire again ?

ON THE ROAD.

Her veil is soft as a summer-cloud;
And when she passes, the flowers are sad
That they cannot follow her.

ONE can see the road from the river's edge;
    Always I look along the road,
For down it something always comes
Towards me, something that doth smile,
    And something that doth weep.
It is a woman, and a child.
And the weeping woman faster goes
Than doth the smiling child.
And both would give a drink to me,
But the woman doth fetch the water up,
    And handeth me the pitcher full,
        Quicker than doth the little child.
The pitcher's rim is broken.
Then both go hence—and I only think
    Of the woman that weeps—but I forget,
    Always forget, the smiling child,
        Because it did not still my thirst;
        And every day I go and watch
            The road, to see them coming.

Her veil is soft as a summer-cloud;
And when she passes, the flowers are sad
Because they cannot follow.

CRADLE SONG.

THE wind came flying through my chamber,
And when he saw me, he was joyful,
   Because I looked on thee.
Thou didst not heed the wind's rejoicing,
For thou wert hearkening to my song.

   I will sing to thee
   Of the soldier-host
That yestereven marched hence to war,
And to whom with homage we bade farewell.
The earth was proud to feel their footsteps,
The sunshine proud to be their sunshine.
Thou too shalt be a soldier, child,
So that thy land may love and bless thee.
The corn upon the fields grows fairer
   When rain hath fallen,
Yet blood the earth hath need of too;
Therefore I give thee to the earth.
Thou wilt become so brave a soldier,
That even the mountain, to behold thee,
Will one day draw her veil of mist aside.
And o'er thy lot I will not sorrow,

Nor mourn the days thou didst not live.
O Earth, I give my child to thee!

When thou shalt see thy foe lie dying,
Thy thoughts will turn toward Death, and kindly
Thou wilt look back, and tenderly, on Life,
    Since Death is in thy thoughts.
Along white roadways thou shalt travel,
    Whereon men thirst,
      Beneath the tent lie down at even
        In bitter cold.
Glorious thy lot will be—yea, even
    Like to the eagle's and the sun's;
Men raise their heads when they would look at them.
Thou mayst not think of maidens' girdles,
    Nor of their eyes,
      And thou shalt say to them:
        "I must go hence."
For thou wilt be a soldier, O my child!

The wind came flying through my chamber,
And when he saw me he was joyful,
    Because I looked on thee.
Thou didst not heed the wind's rejoicing,
For thou wert hearkening to my song.

STILLBORN.

Amid the springing grain flowers, too, spring up,
Therefore they drink the dew
That the sky sends upon the springing grain.
The threshold of the cottage was all wet
Because last night such heavy dew hath fallen.

WOMAN! take up thy life once more
    Where thou hast left it;
Nothing is changed for thee, thou art the same,
    Thou, who didst think
That all things would be wholly changed for thee.
No dirge doth echo through thy dwelling-place;
    One cannot mourn as dead
    That which hath never lived.
Yet had I made for him a dirge so sweet!
Telling therein, that he was all thy hope,
    And that he did not well
To go ere he had looked upon the world—
    To think so ill of what he ne'er had seen.
Woman! while thou didst bear him, hast thou ever
Told him of graves? or spoken of the sorrow
Of barren wombs?

Didst thou not tell him of thy womb's rejoicing
    Over his life ?
And that spring sometimes comes upon this earth,
And that some souls there are, that do remember ?
Nay, thou didst think on sorrow
While thou hadst joy within thee ;
    And sorrow frightened him.
Thou didst not tell him, that thy cottage-windows
    Looked toward the plain ;
That rivers love the flowers upon their banks,
And that the storks come home ;
That there are birds that sing, and men as well,
And that their songs are sweet.
Nay, but thou spak'st to him of graves, and so
Their rest grew dear to him.
Now can I make no tender dirge o'er him.
    I never saw him live.
Return thee to thy hearth,
And think of him before thine empty hearth ;
Saying, while thou dost muse of him :
    " How empty is my hearth ! "
Toward thy husband stretch thou forth thy hand
    With gentle smile, that he
May smile again, and think of Death no more.
    For Death it was not
That passed through this thy house—but it was Life
That would not take up her abode therein.
Thou didst but ask him from afar :

" Wilt thou indeed be mine ? "—
  As one may ask the stars.
The stars reply : " Nay, we belong to no one."
Thou didst but say to him from far :
  " I love thee ! "
Even as one may say it to the sky.
The sky makes answer : " Nay, the love of men
  Is nought to me ! "
Go, woman, to thy daily work again—
Nothing is changed for thee.

Amid the sprouting seeds flowers, too, are growing,
And so they drink the rain
That the sky sends upon the sprouting grain.
The threshold of thy cottage is so wet
Because last night such heavy dew hath fallen.

The moon, she is a maiden's heart,
   And love once dwelt therein,
Ah, in those days the maiden's heart
   Was sunshine through and through ;
But when love left the maiden's heart,
   'Twas then that it grew pale.
And Heaven took it up on high,
Yet sadly still it looketh down
Upon the earth, where love did dwell,
   And paler grows the while.

The moon, she fears the sunshine sore,
Because the sunshine knows full well
     Wherefore the moonlight is so pale.

The rivers say, when she appears :
   " O little maid's pale heart,
Come, rest in us ! " and in their sleep
   The birds all say to her :
" Come, go to sleep in our nests with us ! "
   The grave saith : " Maiden's heart,
Pale heart, make me grow paler too ! "
And everything to slumber turns
   That so that heart may sleep.
Yet though she see them slumb'ring all,
   She slumbers not, nor nods her head,
But stands and watches Sleep.

THE MOON.

A green, green tree in my courtyard stands,
  The sunshine loves it, the breezes rock it ;
But when snow hath fallen, the tree forgetteth
  That April once was here.

THE moon, she fears the sunshine sore,
Because the sunshine knows full well
    Wherefore the moonlight is so pale.
The moon is loth that the sun should tell
Her secret ; and she hides away
When the sun comes forth, that so, perchance,
    The sunshine may forget.
But I am brother to the sun,
    He telleth me his secrets all—
    How he hath taught the birds to sing,
    The ears of corn to turn to gold,
    The forests to grow green.
And thus he hath betrayed to me
    Wherefore the moon is pale.

THE TWO KNIVES.

White blossoms hath the acacia-tree,
  My necklet hath blue beads.
The Cobzar's voice goes echoing through the night.

Two gleaming knives my brother had,
  That, glistening, on the wall hung crossed;
  And why he loved those knives so well
      I could not ever think.

When down into the river cool
  The sun hath sunk, the plain grows red.
And if my Love had love for me,
  All my life long I'd sing thereof,
      And spin him shirts so fine.

When in the chamber night is black,
I hear the knives that talk together.
One saith: "'Twas I that pierced the wife;"
The other: "I that killed the husband."
Saith one: "Such lukewarm blood had she,
Like eggs beneath the mother's wing!"
The other: "Such red blood had he,
      As red as wine in glass!"

" And whosoe'er would reach that house
   Must wade the river through.
The house, it knew not that we came
   To kill that man and wife.
Her white veil round her head she wore,
   Bracelets were on her arm,
She listened to the river's flow,
   And with it her last hour flowed by.

And ever since that time, the souls
Of wife and husband hither come,
   At night, to curse us both.
They say : ' Why gleam ye on the wall,
   Crossed on the wall, ye knives,
   What have ye done with that our blood ?'—
Then we make answer to the souls :
   ' The river washed the blood away,
   The river hurries hence.'—
' What have ye done with our blood ?' they ask—
—' We dried it in the sun, and yet
   The sun is shining still.'—
' What have ye done with our blood ?' they ask—
—' We drank it, and we gleam ! ' "

White blossoms bath the acacia-tree,
   My necklet bath blue beads.
The Cobzar's singing echoes through the night.

THE SPRING.

The snow has fallen, and we shall not find
The path that leads unto the huts again,
Yet we look up and see the clear blue sky,
From whence the snow has fallen.

I CHARGE thee, drink no water from that spring,
    Thy soul would burn;
For in the evening late, the maiden's soul
    Did drink therefrom.
Snow-white the soul is, and it thirsteth ever.
    "Happy are ye," it saith unto the flowers,
    "That every night drink dew!"
And to the rivers, too, it saith: "Ah me,
    The plains are happy, for ye water them."
Then to the spring the soul draws nigh, lamenting
    That it must pine so sore,
And saith: "I surely thought to still my thirst
    There in the grave,
But Death is arid, so I have come back."

And when two lovers chance to meet that soul
    The while it drinks,
They too for ever thirsting will remain,

And down into the grave, to still that thirst,
　　They too will go.

I charge thee, drink no water from that spring,
For in the evening late, the maiden's soul
　　Doth drink therefrom.

The snow has fallen, and we shall not find
　　The path that leads back to the huts again.
Yet we look up and see the clear blue sky,
　　From whence the snow has fallen.

THE SONG OF THE YOUNG MAIDEN.

A star hath fallen on the spot
Where thou art singing—
Thy bracelets' ringing
Keeps all the birds awake.

Thou that dost watch o'er children's sleep
    And gently rockest them,
Thy voice is dear to sucking babes,
    The aged love thy voice;
Come now and sing a song for me,
    Thy voice, I love it too;
Yea, like the river's rippling sound
    As through the maize it flows,
Or like the poplar's whispering
    That by my threshold grows.
Sing me the song of the young, young maid,
    That bids her spindle dance, and sets
        Her heart a-dancing too.—

A horseman rode across the ford,
    Into the water fell his sword.
What would become of the maiden's heart
    Once empty of its love?

What will the swordless horseman do?
I lay and drank at the water's edge,
  The sword came swimming by me;
I thrust it into my girdle fast,
And dear is the weight of the sword to me,
  It sings me songs of battle.
  Horseman that wentest through the ford,
Wouldest thou fain get back thy sword?
  Then come and sit thee down by me,
  Beneath my threshold's poplar-tree.
There dance my heart and spindle both,
  Because the sword of the fight doth tell;
I will give it thee back, but yet I trow
  Thy thoughts are all of my spindle now!

I have sung the song of the young, young maid.

    A star hath fallen on the spot
    Where thou art singing—
    Thy bracelets' ringing
    Keeps all the birds awake.

THE WIDOW.

The sun is hidden far behind the willows ;
The willows shivered, for they hid the sun.

IF a knock sounded on my door at even,
    First I should think that it was him returning,
But soon I should remember he was dead,
    And know it was his dear soul home returning ;
Then should I bid it enter at the door
    And come close, close beside me.
And his dear soul would ask me :
" The children, and the maize-fields, and the cattle,
    How fare they all ? "
And I would answer his dear soul : " All well ; "
    That it might rest and fall asleep in peace.
Yet would I not, that his dear soul should ask me :
    " How fares it with the sorrow of thy soul ? "
For since unto the dead one may not lie,
I must perforce give answer : " 'Tis not healed."
    . Then his dear soul
    Never again could fall asleep in peace.
    Moreover, his dear soul will surely ask
For flowers of me, and I will give it flowers,
    Yet would I not, it asked me for a drink,

For one can give the dead no drink save tears,
   And I would not it should perceive that these
     Were tears of mine.
Then his dear soul
   Were fain to see our children, and the house,
To know if all were yet unchanged, and I
   Would show him house and children, for they all
     Are yet unchanged.
Yet would I not, that his dear soul should ask me
   To show my face—quick-sighted are the dead,
And he would see my face all drawn with sorrow.
Ah no ! for when upon the door at even
   His dear soul knocketh,
I must be able thus to answer him :
   "All here within goes well—yea, in my heart,
     And on my face ;
I have forgotten thee, go hence and sleep
   In peace again,"—for ne'er the dead must weep—
     "All here goes well."
Then his dear soul would wend its way again
   Back to the grave, nor turn to look behind ;
And never more would his dear soul arise
   To knock upon my door at eventide.

    The sun is hidden far behind the willows ;
    The willows shivered, for they hid the sun.

THE FLOWER-CHILD.

(OR FOUNDLING.)

To-day is Sunday, come away and dance!
I passed the lads anon, and they were singing.
The forest said: "Oh hearken, how they sing!"

SHE will not come to-morrow,
Nor came she yesterday,
She who could end the stranger's life I lead.
Perhaps I meet her every day,
And she doth turn away her face
To hide her tears from me; for if I saw
That she was weeping, straightway I should cry:
　　"Lo, this is she!"
She turns away from me her face
That she my sorrow may not see,
For if she saw my sadness, then
She never could refrain from crying:
　　"Thou art my child!"
Perhaps she sees me standing at his side,
And dares not say: "That is thy father!"
For fear that I might hate him,
And, with him, hate her too.

Yet both I love, even as the flower its root.
I curse them not—I say to them in dreams :
" Blessed be the hour, wherein ye loved each other."
And never would I tell them of my sorrows.
And if they asked concerning them,
I would reply : "But I am happy !
And to the graves I never go ;
The graves beguile me not."
This would I tell them, and my sorrow
Within my heart's depths I would hide,
As rain in hollow stones is hidden,
As one who dies, doth hide the secret
Of his last suffering and woe.
And those who see me never say :
" How full his heart is ! "—rather all men think
That it is empty, empty quite, my heart.
I love the happy children of the mothers,
Because I hear them say : " My mother ! "—
I listen, that I too may learn to say it,
And when I am alone, repeat it low.
But when I say it, 'tis as though I had
A different voice from them, the mothers' children,
For whom the mothers pray upon their knees,
And weave them shirts so fine, the livelong day,
And sing them off to sleep with lullabies.
O mother, whom perchance I see
In every path, and every day
Washing the hemp beside the river—

If thou wert dead, how would I love thy grave,
How gladly linger by it,
And cover it with flowers,
Not naming thee, but saying:
" I am a son of Earth, and love this grave
Because a little earth doth cover it,
And who it is sleeps here, I do not know."
Oh mother, nay ! thou never canst be dead,
For surely, ere thy death, thou wouldst have called me,
And bidden me love thy grave.
Thou surely wouldst have feared
To be so cold therein
Without thy poor child's love !
Nay, but thou livest, mother;
Then come one evening, while I am asleep,
And look upon my sleep ;
Then in the morning I can say : " At least
She looked upon my sleep."

To-day is Sunday, come away and dance!
I passed the lads anon, and they were singing.
The forest said : " Oh hearken, how they sing ! "

THE HEIDUCK'S FLOWERS.

Look never upon me in my sleep
The while I dream,
For then thou wouldst see upon my face
The smiles of my dream, or else its tears.
The wind hath driven the clouds away.

TO-DAY I waked early, and first of all
I saw the sun, and then the road
Where men went by, with pipe in mouth.
One was a Heiduck, and in his hand
He carried a flower—and his youth it was.
In his mouth he carried another flower—
And his song was that; and another flower
He bore in his girdle—and that was his love.
I went with my spade to dig on the plain,
From the well I drank water,
And looked at the trees ;
And then in the shade of the trees I slept.
And at even I came to my house again,
I saw the moon rise as I went ;
And again on the road I saw men pass by,
One was the Heiduck.
                    A faded flower

He bore in his hand—and that was his youth.
In his mouth he carried a faded flower—
And that was his song.

                And a faded flower
He bore in his girdle—and that was his love.
I bade him not enter my dwelling-place ;
He went on through the darkening night.

Look never upon me in my sleep
    The while I dream,
For then thou wouldst see upon my face
The smiles of my dream, or the tears of my dream.
The wind hath driven the clouds away.

THE ROAD TO PRISON.

Onward floweth the water, onward through meadows broad;
" How happy," the meadows say, "art thou, to be rippling
*   onward."*
And my heart is beating, beating, beneath my girdle here;
" O heart," the girdle saith, "how happy art thou, that
*   thou beatest!"*

THE road that I tread, is not dusty from wanderers' foot-
    steps,
Nor from the oxen, that go their way to the ploughing,
        Nor from the passing of lovers—
Nay, but the footsteps of prisoners have left the road full
    of dust,
And the clang of their chains hath brought sorrow to all
    the trees by the way;
The clang of those chains the trees never more can forget,
Nor can they in their prison yonder, forget the trees and
    their sorrow.
And there in the way the prisoners met the young maiden,
    And they wept when they saw her so young—
And the maiden gave drink to them all, and went hence
    with their blessing.

They thought of their houses, that over them wept, and
    of those
        Who wept in the houses.
And the dust of the road, and the scorching fire of the sun,
They felt them no more, the while they thought on these
    things ;
They strained their ear to catch the song of the birds,
      The last they might hear for so long ;
And they blessed the birds, because they had been the last
      To sing on their way.
So wearily went they hence, as though all their life they
    must wander,
      And already had wandered for long.
To the men they did meet they said : " And yet we are
    all your brothers ; "
      And the clang of their chains went with them.
And one on his brow yet bore the tears of his mother,
Another the kiss of his wife—and the brows were all
    darkened alike.
Yet each one smiled, as though he would say : " See, I
    smile ! "
They dreaded the threshold, awaiting them there at the
    end ;
Yet were they in haste to o'erstep it, and hide from the day
      Their weariful smile and their chains.
And over the threshold, one following another, they stepped,
And the first one that crossed it, did envy the last, for
    that he

Had yet to o'erstep it.
Of their homes they thought, and their sins, yet they
sorrowed more deeply
For their homes than for all their sins.
Their dreams were distraught with anguish, and each one,
awakening,
Would say to his fellow: "I know not whereof I have
dreamed—
I dreamed that so white was the road, and that prisoners'
footsteps
Had left the road full of dust."

Onward floweth the water, onward through meadows broad,
" How happy," the meadows say, " art thou, to be rippling
onward ! "
And my heart is beating, beating, beneath my girdle here ;
" O heart," the girdle saith, " how happy art thou, that
thou beatest ! "

THE SOLDIER'S WIFE.

Know'st thou what the harvest-fields are saying?
" We have loved the sunshine all too dearly;
Therefore now they mow us down, for loving
The sunshine over-much."

HE slept beneath the lime-tree, and it looked upon his
    sleep.
Fresh from the battle he had come, and home with him
    he brought
The scent of blood upon his clothes; and all the flowers
    were sad
Because the wind loved that the best,
    Better than all their scents.
Ah! soldier, thou young soldier, coming from the battle,
Thou didst not see me going by, with the rustling of ripe
    grass,
For thou wert lost in dreaming only of the battle,
And dearer is thy sword to thee than any glance of mine.
The eagle loves the sunshine better than his eyrie,
And dark the hut would seem to thee after the glee of
    fight,
The joy of breaking like a storm over the fields of dead.
And dearer is thy wound to thee, than any kiss of mine.

Now wilt thou yet require of me, that I our son should
    give thee,
To join the hosts of war.
Thy courser speeds as swiftly, as clouds before the storm-
    wind,
And scarcely have our women the time to reach their
    threshold,
To see him flying onward, or ever he is gone.
But thou no more dost love it, the quietness of the thres-
    hold ;
    Thou lov'st thy sword, he knows it,
And as for love of women, he biddeth thee forget it,
    And saith : " Touch not their veil."

When wilt thou be returning to this thy home again ?
The morning marvels not to find thee,
The evening saith : " What, not yet come ? "
My hand hangs idly rocking the cradle, while I muse
    Upon him in the battle ;
And who will give him drink, I wonder,
And who will lull his sleep, or wailing
Will sing his dirge when he is dead.
The plain is wide, and o'er it the little birds go roaming,
So doth my heart, but thou no longer
Dost love the loving of my heart.
    Thy courser speeds so swiftly,
That e'en the moon can scarcely from out the clouds come
    gliding

In time to see him flying, or ever he is gone.
But thou no more dost love it, the moonlight's restfulness.
And thou upon the earth wilt slumber gladly, thinking
    That it shall be thy grave;
Even as the rain, rejoicing to know that thou shalt sink
    Down into earth.
My voice is dumb and silent, since thine I hear no longer;
My step is slow and heavy, since thine no more I follow;
Nor do I any longer put flowers in my girdle;
    My necklet, too, now slumbers,
Because it hears no longer the beating of my heart.
Thy courser speeds so swiftly, I scarce have time to loosen
My veil to see him flying, or ever he is gone.

Know'st thou what the harvest-fields are saying?
  " We have loved the sunshine all too dearly;
Therefore now they mow us down, for loving
    The sunshine over-much."

MAD.

We shall not see again the foot of the willows
Until the river is low.

I NEVER bade him stay, because it was written,
In my fate it was written, that I should see him go.

And still the fire burns on, as though it could warm me.
To-morrow is Sunday, the peasant-folk will be joyful.

Then do not think, that I bade him stay beside me ;
He went—but he returned, and returns every evening.—
Sit by the fire, draw closer yet, belovèd ;
Thou art not as cold as I, it still can warm thee.
I am so cold, dost see, that to me it is nothing,
    For I am always cold.
Ah ! but how good thou wert to return, my belovèd,
To return to me—and which was the way that thou
        camest ?
Was it there, where beside the road the mill-wheel is
        singing ?
Or down by the path all enwreathed with the raspberry-
        bushes,
The boughs that have reddened ;my lips with their beauti-
        ful berries ?

But, nay! how good thou art to return, my belovèd!
And if the dead should return, one would say to them
     surely:
" How good ye are to return! "—yet I love thee far better
Than all my dead over whom I lament with sore weeping.
How good thou art, that thou livest, nor lettest me
     weep.
And know, that the moon, too, is here, and her stars
     without number;
I love thee far better than them, nor do look at them ever
The while thou art with me, but lo! when thou leavest
     me, straightway
I look at them then, and of thee we hold converse together.
I lighted the fire, for I knew that thou wouldest be coming,
And beside it with thee I sit whispering, whispering softly.
Then my sorrow flies hence;—but I put the fire out when
     thou goest.
"For wherefore, indeed, should I burn without him?"
     saith the fire.
When thou comest again, take the path by the raspberry-
     bushes,
Inquire not thy way of another, nor ask of another
To give thee a drink—nay, ask of no other woman,
     Keep all thy thirst for me.
The other women, they have their veils [1] and their spindles.
What song shall I choose? what song wilt thou have me
     sing thee?

[1] Note 1.

The river went by and bore hence the tears of the widow.
The leaves of the nut-trees will soon be sere in the forest ;
And I am young and yet old, and I waken pity.
Yet why have men pity upon me—since I am so happy ?
I lighted the fire, for I knew that thou wouldest be coming.

We shall not see again the foot of the willows
Until the river is low.

GIPSY SONG.

WITH trembling hand I touched the shift's white fold,
The beads of blue that clasped thy neck about.
Before my tent the fire burnt bright of old ;
    See now —the fire is out.

Beneath the hill, at witching eventide,
Thou gavest me thy fresh, sweet lips of yore ;
My heart within my breast for gladness cried ;
    Hark now—it beats no more.

As o'er the grass, beneath the poplars there,
We gaily stepped, the high noon overhead,
Then Love was born—was born so strong and fair.
    Knowest thou ?—Love is dead.

Because thy soul was dark, to evil turned,
Therefore it was Love had no power to hold.
Before my tent the fire once brightly burned ;
    See now—the fire is cold.

THE WATER OF PRAYER.

Go not forth at the time the flowers are sleeping,
The flowers mislike that one should watch their sleep.

EVERY morning
There came a child, and set without my door
A pitcher filled, and said: "Oh! pray for her,
Oh! pray for her, the while ye drink this water."
"And is her grave already green?" I asked;
The child made answer: "Nay, it still is young."
I looked among the graves until I found
The youngest grave—and then I prayed for her,
    The while I drank that water.

Go not forth at the time the flowers are sleeping,
For flowers mislike that one should watch their sleep.

NO SON.

The furrows my oxen draw are the straightest of all;
And in my belt I carry so many knives
That they girdle my waist about.
The rain doth bid the birds fly home to their nests.

I HAD a dream, that at last thou wert born to me,
Thou for whom 'tis so hard to be born to me.
That was a waking dream that I dreamed, at noon,
With eyes fixed long on the furrows all full of seed.
Some shoots already were breaking forth from the furrows,
      And said: "We, we are born!"—
Then did I envy my field for its fatherhood;
It seemed to me, as though I were now the father
Of a brave, strong son, who was setting forth for the
      battle—
And I wept at parting, yet gloried over the fight.
And then it seemed to me that I was the father
Of a shepherd-lad, who drove his flock to the mountains;
I saw the mountain smiling upon my shepherd,
And saw that the heart of the shepherd was smiling too—
      And I rejoiced.
Then it seemed to me that I was a father's father;
I saw the children greeting him on his threshold,

And the kindliness of that greeting filled my soul,
And all his house, too, overflowed with it,
And like a sun, his joy shone forth to me.
But the real sun sank down beneath the furrows,
And I seemed to myself the father of my sorrow,
 And of my loneliness.
These to my hut I carried back with me,
 And to my wife I spake:
"Wife, we are all alone and full of sorrow!"
Silent was she, for she knew not how to answer ;
Silent were both our hearts, for they were empty.
Then of all loneliness, and pain, and sorrow
 I felt myself the father—
The son of the graves I felt myself, and the husband
Of yon dumb woman, whose womb would be silent ever,
 As were our hearts.
Then, that we might forget, we looked at the furrows,
All full of seed—and some shoots already were breaking
Forth from the furrows, and said: "We, we are born!"
Nor did one of us ask the other: "Whereon art thou
 looking?"—
We only looked at the growing seeds together.

The furrows my oxen draw are the straightest of all;
* And in my belt I carry so many knives*
* That they girdle my waist about.*
The rain doth bid the birds fly home to their nests.

AUTUMN SONG.

The birds have flown, because the mists were falling ;
As night drew on, I saw them passing by.
The fire burns bright and louder howls the wind,
The wind is sad because he is so cold.

UPON my leathern belt thy hand was resting,
  I felt it touch my knife.
I told thee then to let my heart sleep on ;
  My heart needs rest so sorely.
But yet those eyes of thine, they would not suffer
  My heart to sleep in peace ;
Thou saidst to me, that thou perchance might'st die—
And then I pictured how thy death would be,
And felt that at the very thought thereof
  My heart grew sad—as sad as wandering birds
    When mists are falling.
The burden of thee is most dear to Earth,
    Therefore thou must not die.
But if thou didst, the whole wide world would wish
To die, and be a sharer in thy death.
Thy grave would draw me to it and entice me,
Beside thy gravestone I should sit me down,
    Or roam around thy house,

To see thy dear soul roaming round the house.
Then to thy soul I would cry out: "Oh! stay,
Oh! stay by me," with such a strength of love,
That strong thy soul need be to break away.
But know, the soul that wanders round a house
    Is never happy.
Thou wouldst not that thy soul should be unhappy?
Then stay thou here on earth; for see, the stars
    Are all too far for thee.
And even the stars, too, must be glad to feel
They have a little sister here on earth.
Come, touch my knife, that I may be a hero,
    But never touch my heart,
For then it will not sleep, and human hearts
    Must sleep, that they may live.

The birds have flown, because the mists were falling;
  As night drew on, I saw them passing by.
The fire burns bright and louder howls the wind,
  The wind is sad because he is so cold.

SLEEP.

Beneath the poplars by my door
  Didst sit thee down,
And on my door didst look, but never enter.
Why dost thou love the poplars' shade so much?

SLEEP said : " I know so many things ;
  Dreams do I know, and sighs.
More than the forest that ceaseless murmurs,
More than the river that weeps, I know,
  More than the wind that sings.
And I know more than the hearts of men,
  Since I can silence their hearts."
So then the forest, the wind, and the river,
And the hearts of men, all said to Sleep :
" Come, tell us what thou dost know."
Then Sleep replied : "I will tell you softly."—
And he said to them : " Rest I know.
And I know, besides, what the maiden hideth—
What the wife doth not dare to tell ;
From the breath of their lips I guess it.
Death envies me, for whoso would find me,
He need not go down to the grave.
And Death speaks thus to me : ' Why dost thou let them

Awaken again?' But I let men awaken
That they may hold me more dear.
And I lay a smile on their lips, moreover,
Instead of the tears they have shed.
'Thou hast the face of my heart's belovèd,'
The maiden saith to me; and the wife:
'The voice of my husband hast thou.'
Death suffereth me to seek through the graves,
And bring forth those who long have slept
　　To those who sleep but an hour.
And those who sleep but an hour, they bless me
For giving back those who for long have slept.
'Thou hast the taste of the freshest water,'
The thirsting traveller saith to me.
'Thou hast the look of my home,' saith the wand'rer.
And in his shade the Past doth let me
Seek those who have suffered sore, and bring them
Up before those who made them suffer;
And those who made them suffer, tremble
At sight of those who have suffered sore.
'Lo! thou hast blood upon thy hand!'
Saith the man who hath stained his knife, to me.
'Thou hast a dagger in thy hand,'
Saith the man who hath betrayed, to me.
I am so gentle, yet so dread,
That all mankind is fain to have me,
Because they love me and yet fear.
I dwell in nests, since they are lofty;

Luteplayer's Songs.

In graves, because grass covers them.
And the hearts of men have need of me;
And I have need of their joys and sorrows
    To fashion dreams of them.
And he who lies asleep is sacred.
Men say of one who sleeps: 'Heaven loves him;
    For see, he sleeps.'
But he who cannot sleep, arouses
Uneasiness in all men's hearts,
    They say of him, 'He cannot sleep.'"

Beneath the poplars by my door
    Didst sit thee down,
And on my door didst look, yet never enter.
Why dost thou love the poplars' shade so much?

FORGOTTEN.

At the tree's foot a hay-fork hath been left,
And all day long it hears the birds a-singing.
Beside the mill grows thyme.

I AM forgotten—
And if the sun doth glance in through my window,
I am amazed that he remembers me.
The grass but grows from custom in my field,
I too from custom let my spindle dance.
The road that leadeth to my house, doth hear
The echo of no footstep.   And the morning
Saith to me: "Thou art the forgotten one."
He whom I loved, he took his horse, his mantle,
And, singing, rode from hence.
                              At night I dream
I see him ride through river and through forest
Until he reaches a great village.   There
At the third hut he stops,
And on the threshold waits for him a maiden;
The maiden speaks: "Thou from afar that comest,
Riding through streams and forests,
Hast thou no wife, far off in distant lands,
Who sorely mourns for thee ?"—

He answers: "I have none." And then the maiden
Doth smile on him, and he beside her tarries.
Anon he takes his horse once more, and cometh
Unto another village, and there stops
At the third hut, wherein men laughing drink.
And the men give him drink, and ask him, saying:
" Is there not one thou dost the while remember,
In emptying this glass ?"
He answers: "There is no one."
Again he mounts his horse and comes a-riding
Through a wide meadow, full of naught but stones ;
At the third stone he stays,
And there beside the third stone standeth One,
Her arms outstretched toward him,
And asketh him: "Or ever thou embrace me,
Say, is there no one thou wouldst fain embrace ?"
He answers: "There is no one."
For surely, the forgotten one am I—
And he I love, can ne'er remember me.
The earth remembers not the golden maize
When it is cut. The sky forgets the cloud ;
The furrows, even, do forget the rain.
And if the sun doth glance in through my window,
I am amazed that he remembers me.

> *At the tree's foot a hay-fork hath been left,*
> *And all day long it bears the birds a-singing.*
> *Thyme grows beside the mill.*

TO THE MAIDEN.

I weep because the wind is sighing,
But thou, thou singest in the sun.
Two little birds came past us flying—
Why I am weeping, asketh one;
The other asks why thou art singing;
One answer makes the sky: " In sooth,
For very wantonness of youth ! "

Oh ! do not ever from a grave pluck flowers,
The dead have naught but flowers left to-day,
   The while our youth is ours.
Thy hand is toying with thy necklet gay ;
And all the boughs—their little nests have they.

Oh ! let no laugh the graves' deep silence break,
Silence alone is left unto the dead.
   Thy belt six turns doth make [1]
About thy waist.   And when didst bend thy head
To drink—" Oh, drink again ! " the river said.

Tell not the graves, how fair are the spring days,
Forgetfulness is all the dead have here.
   I shut thine eyes' deep gaze
Within my very soul's recesses, dear ;
Thy spindle's whirring ceaseless fills mine ear.   .

       [1] Note 2.

The threshold of thy house I love to tread,
The threshold smiles amid its flowers at me.
    But do not tell the dead
That Love endureth, and may constant be.
They never would believe or list to thee.

    I weep because the wind is sighing,
    But thou, thou singest in the sun.

THE SONG OF THE CROSS-SISTERS.[1]

Along both of the roads there are copses of nut-trees growing;
    On one they are yet green,
But on the other, their leaves have dropped already—
See, we will take the road where they yet are green.

O SISTER! speak, why didst thou not straightway tell me?
Three distaffs we emptied together, and yet, thy hand—
    I saw it not tremble.
    When I spoke of him
Thou didst bend thy head to drink from the wooden
    pitcher—
    I thought thou wert parched with thirst.
O sister! was it from graves thou didst learn to keep
    silence,
    That thou hast kept silence so?
And dost thou not think that the graves would be far, far
    happier
    If they could only speak?
    When I told thee of him
Thou didst but toy with my girdle's fluttering fringes,
    And I thought thy fingers were idle.
How it is in his dwelling-house, thou hast never asked me,

[1] Note 3.

For hadst thou asked, I straightway had understood thee,
    And known thou didst love him too;
Then with all my heart I had striven not to love him;
But now we love him both, we two together,
And these two loves of ours are even as the river,
That weeps because of its eternal flowing,
    Yet cannot cease to flow.
Now I begin to hate thee, and thou art hateful
    In all thou dost, to me;
I cannot hear my thoughts for thy spindle's whirring,
And my heart, what time it hears thee singing, deemeth
    Thou singest but a dirge.
We glance at each other, whene'er he comes towards us,
    To mark which hoped for him most;
And she hath smiling lips, to whom he shows favour,
But knives beneath her eyes the other beareth.
And when he goeth hence, we glance at each other,
    To mark which sorrows most.

THE CROSS-SISTER.

O sister! sister! of glass so white are thine ear-rings,
And when thou dancest, upon the face they caress thee;
    Then fain would I dance by thee.
But now I am fain to see thee dead, yet am fearful
Lest thou shouldst die, for then he might weep for thee,
And then I should know, it was thee alone that he
    lovèd;

And if that be so indeed, I will not know it.
The tree knows naught of the axe that shall come to
    fell it,
    And rejoiceth in the sun.—
If I ask of thee, why thou wearest so many a necklet,
    No answer thou givest me.
But every day I seem to see thee grow fairer,
And fear that thou, indeed, art she whom he loveth,
And that it is thy heart's rejoicing makes thee
    So passing fair.
The wool upon thy spindle doth seem far whiter;
And when beside the well I see thee standing,
    I ask: "Why stands she there?"
Fearing, lest thou be there but to await him.
Nor am I even at rest when thou art sleeping,
Because thou surely in thy dreams must see him,
And he, perchance, in dreams doth say he loves thee,
When my image is not there to say: "Thou liest."
O sister, sister! when didst thou grieve thy mother,
Or I forget to give drink to the thirsty wand'rer,
That God now sends such punishment upon us?
Far rather would I die with no holy taper,
Or see from off my cottage wall to-morrow
    The flowers wiped away,[1]
Than have a sorrow, that only grows more heavy
    When it is shared with thee.
Nay! I would bless the woman who would sing me

[1] Note 4.

Dirges upon my threshold, that Death might take me
    Within a month away.
And yet I will not die, for he would not sorrow ;
Then should I surely know he loveth thee.

Along both of the roads there are copses of nut-trees growing ;
    On one they are yet green,
But on the other, their leaves have fall'n already—
See, we will take the road where they yet are green.

DIRGE OF A MOTHER OVER HER SON.

I saw a floweret on the meadow—
It grew among the new-mown hay;
The golden maize was not so fair,
Yet, seeing that flower, the little birds all wept.
Thou floweret on the meadow,
How comest thou among the new-mown hay?

Cast down thy mantle,
Down by the road-side here;
Cast down thy sickle,
There, on the other side,
And get thee home! Go home—
Stay not upon the bridge,
Stay not beside the well,
And stay not at the crossways.

So I went home.
I found the door half-open,
And the door spake: "Not from the wind that bloweth!"
I found the chamber darkened;
The chamber spake: "Not because night hath fallen!"
Then I remembered yonder little flower.
I saw thee sleep—

And understood right well
That yonder little flower was thy soul,
That sent me to thy body,
And I was not to stay upon the bridge,
 Nor stay beside the well,
  Nor loiter at the crossways.
  Yet had I known
 That yonder little flower was thy soul,
I gladly would have stayed by it awhile;
 Only thy soul was fain
  Quickly to consummate its blossoming,
  And therefore sent me hence
 That so it might not have to take its flight
 Before my very eyes.

And here am I—what willest thou of me?
 Lo, nothing any more!
What knowledge now is thine?
 A deeper one than ours.
Where art thou going, thus, without us all?
And which of us hath ere forsaken thee,
That thou shouldst so forsake us?
Hast thou not ever shared our water with us,
And wilt not now share Death?
What will the seeds be saying
Thou didst entrust to Earth,
When they come forth and find thee here no more?
Beneath thy casement, see, the maidens pass,

The river passeth too ;
And on the morrow is a festival ;
Hast told thy grave thereof ?
Perchance, if thou hadst told it,
The grave had left thee to enjoy the Day
    For that one day.
And didst thou tell thy grave thou hadst a mother ?
For she, the mother of all flowers and harvests,
    Had surely felt some pity.
Nay, rather hast thou told the Earth, perchance,
    That we are rich in tears,
And since the Earth was dry and lacked refreshment,
She took thee hence that she might drink our tears.
Ah, but thou didst not tell her
    That bitter are our tears,
Or she had feared to taste such bitterness,
    And ne'er had taken thee.

    See, here am I—
Yet dost thou not so much as raise thy head.
One hour already have I cried to thee,
And yet shall cry for many weary hours.
    See, here am I, yea, here !
But it is naught to thee that I have come,
And stayed not on the bridge,
Nor stayed beside the well,
Nor loitered at the crossways.
    See, I am here !

I saw a floweret on the meadow—
It grew among the new-mown hay ;
The golden maize was not so fair,
Yet, seeing that flower, the little birds all wept.
Thou floweret on the meadow,
How camest thou among the new-mown hay ?

THE SONG OF THE OLD WELL.

Thou too wilt soon go hence from me once more,
Oh thou, who camest once to me before ;
My threshold will see my sorrow, and it will know
That I am weeping for that thou didst go.

I SLEEP, yet I love to be wakened, and love to see
The fresh young faces bending over me,
And the faces of them that are old, I love them too,
For those as well in the days of their youth I knew.
The song of the wind in the trees, and the voice of the bird,
I hear them not—and yet 'tis as though I heard,
For I feel that the birds are singing, there on high,
And I feel that above the strong wind bloweth by.
I sleep, yet I love to be wakened, day by day,
For I am the comforter, here beside the way ;
A welcome sight to the weary wand'rer's eye,
As to the maidens, who at eve draw nigh
To sing their songs to me—and I know them well,
Yea, all their songs—and all their dreams could tell.
Whoso is tired, I love his weariness,
And I love the wand'rer's grief of heart no less,
Who comes from far.   The thirst of the herds I love,
And to hear the pipe of the shepherd's flute above.

G

And he who fain would wake me from my sleep
Must stoop him down to me, for I am deep,
But yet, when one doth speak to me, his quest
I answer from the depths of my deep breast.
I love the moss that round my brink grows green,
Whereon the young folk come and sit, I ween,
And that the maids sometimes, with idle hand,
Stroke gently with their spindles as they stand.
In joy and sorrow, they all of them come to me,
And I welcome them all; for though asleep I be,
I love to be wakened. And something in me doth sleep—
Something I know not, 'tis my soul—so deep
That none can draw or drink it, for the Earth
It was, that gave my soul, her daughter, birth.
My soul in my depths doth sleep, and it is she
Who maketh answer, when they awaken me.

Thou too wilt soon go hence from me once more,
Oh thou, who camest once to me before;
My threshold will see my sorrow, and it will know
That I am weeping for that thou didst go.

MOTHERS' TEARS.

On the bank beside the ditch he laid his mantle,
That he might sleep the whole long night therein.
Didst thou give water to the oxen yonder?
For they were sore athirst.

I LAID me down in the grass, where it was trackless;
Then a woman came by through the grass and spake to
     me:
"Canst thou tell, where lies the path?"
I said to the woman: "I know not." And she replied:
"Never yet have I found a path beneath my feet,
And the villages always are far away from me;
I never can reach a threshold, and even the graves
  Are always far off from me."—
Then I asked: "Did thy womb bring forth a son, or a
     daughter?"
And she answered: "A son it was came forth from my
     womb;
Since then my husband has shunned me, and I went forth,
Forth to the plains—and my child hears my voice no more;
But upon his father he smiles.
I was fain to hinder his smiling—and wept over him,
Yea, covered his face with my tears.

Since then the child is accursed, for a mother's tears
Weigh heavily on her children—the child is accursed.
And lo! the child has cursed me too, for my weeping,
    So then I fled forth o'er the plain."

> *On the bank beside the ditch he laid his mantle,*
> *That he might sleep the whole long night therein.*
> *Didst thou give water to the oxen yonder?*
>   *For sore athirst were they.*

THE LAST DAY.

When thou hast passed her by
And seest her no more,
I will tell thee who she is,
And thou wilt grieve to hear ;
Thou wilt not turn again to look upon her.

I CAN so well remember
That, thy last day on earth.
So well do I remember,
That everyone keeps saying :
" Why dost thou think of it ? "
And every day that dawneth
I see, as on that day,
The sunshine in my chamber ;
And every day that dawneth
Is like that day to me.
Since then have all my days
Belonged but to the grave—
Even as of yore, to earth
Each of thy days belonged ;
But that one day alone,
That thou didst live for me.
It was thy last, I knew it,

And so I took it all;
Nor would suffer thee, a moment
To look upon the courtyard,
And the apple-trees in blossom,
Or to glance toward the plain;
Nor to gaze upon the faces
That thou so soon wert leaving;
But I came and stood before thee,
And said: "To them thy life,
Thy whole life, hath belongèd,
     This, thy last day, I take!"
And thou didst not weep nor sorrow,
Thou didst answer: "It is well;"
And that day, for me didst live it
     With all thy heart.
This I remember ever.
I knew the grave was waiting,
But I bade it wait a while.
There was something on our threshold
That watched with fierce impatience
The setting of the sun.
And One called out upon me:
"See there, the sun is setting!"
And as the sun sank down
Thou hadst lived out for me
That, thy last day on earth;
And thy first night of death
Belongs to our first sorrow.

Now to the grave, to-morrow,
And all the endless future,
For ever doth belong.
The grave said : " I have finished—
Everything have I taken,
Now therefore I may close."

When thou hast passed her by,
And seest her no more,
I will tell thee who she is,
And thou wilt grieve to hear.
Thou wilt not turn again
  To look upon her.

HER PITCHER.

Now the sun takes leave of us—and after him, as he goeth,
We gaze, and see the plains that sorely mourn his departing ;
It snowed this morning, yonder upon the mountains.

FRESH water my sweetheart hath in her pitcher always,
And on her shoulder beareth the little pitcher,
Tarrying on the way to give drink to all men.
And thus she speaks to each one as he drinketh:
    "In the name of the dead, then, drink."
And when she sleeps in the hut, she leaves on her threshold
    Her pitcher standing.
Then the widow doth go by and drink from the pitcher ;
And there came at night a dead man, too, to drink ;
He spake: "How sweet it is, the maiden's water."
Then the dead man lifted the pitcher upon his shoulder,
And bore it to the graves, that he might extinguish
    The graves' undying thirst ;
And thus the dead man spake to the others, saying :
    "In the name of the living, drink."

Now the sun takes leave of us—and after him, as he goeth,
We gaze, and see the plains that sorely mourn his departing ;
It snowed this morning, yonder upon the mountains.

THE HEART-STEALER.

The moon glides on above the willows gleaming,
And now the willows all night long keep dreaming
Of that, the moon's soft ray.

GIVE me thy heart, O maiden, let me hide it
Where hides my heart, the dagger close beside it
That, 'neath my girdle here, doth keep it warm.

And so thy tender, fluttering heart I'll carry
Far through the night from hence, nor ever tarry,
But o'er the plains and through the forests storm.

And as I pass them like a flash, unheeding,
All men will say: " See yon bold rider speeding,
Who bears from hence his loved one's heart afar."

Thy heart shall feel, in fight, mine thrill with gladness.
I'll show it all the world, its joy and sadness—
Yea, those that weep and those that blessèd are.

The huts, the graves, and all things, I will show them,
Thy tender, fluttering heart shall see and know them,
While thou dost tarry by thy door and say:

"Will he, who stole my heart, be soon returning?"
My steed storms on—thy envious heart is yearning
To see it all, this world so far away;

Nor will return till then—and there's no knowing
But thou wilt have, O maiden, to be going
To fetch it back again thyself some day.

Then to the forest thou wilt say: "Hast spied him,
The rider who bore hence my heart beside him?"
The forest answers: "Hence he bore it fast."—

Then to the plain thou sayest: "Hast thou spied him,
He who went hence and bore my heart beside him?"
The plain replies: "He!—he long since is past!"

Then wilt thou weep—and not thy spindle's dancing,
Thy red, red pinks, thy silver necklet glancing,
Nay, nor the maize fields, e'er could comfort thee

For this thy heart—and therefore thou art keeping
It safely locked within thy bosom sleeping,
Beneath thy girdle, nor wilt give it me;

For well thou know'st, my courser loves his speeding,
And I am one of those who flies unheeding
Along his onward course, that none can stay.

The moon glides on above the willows gleaming,
And now the willows all night long keep dreaming
Of that, the moon's soft ray.

"IT WAS NOT SLEEPING TIME."

Oh, go not forth to-night,
  A star has fallen;
'Twere better thou shouldst wait until the sunrise.
The fragrance of the new-mown hay
  Arises from the plain.

THE child with milk-white teeth
Bore a dagger too near his heart;
And the dagger pierced its way
Deep down to the heart of the child;
The heart fell asleep in its blood.

Then forth from the heart his mother drew the dagger,
But the heart awakened not;
And she said: "Who will give me my child again, or
    beside him
    Lay me in the grave to sleep?"
Yet the heart did never awaken.
Then down in the earth they laid him,
The little child whose heart had fallen asleep;
But as it lay in the earth, behold, it awakened,
And thus it spake: "'Twas not yet time for sleeping;
  Little mother, come tell me why
  I have gone to sleep or ever 'twas time for sleeping.

Had I told thee, then, I was weary,
That thus thou hast put me to sleep?
And wherefore art thou not beside me, little mother,
To sing me lullabies, since I have awakened?
I yearn for thy smile, and for flowers, little mother,
For our dwelling-house, that looketh toward the forest,
For my father, coming home with spade on his shoulder.
  Little mother, oh tell me why
    I have gone to sleep or ever 'twas time for sleeping!"

> *Oh, go not forth to-night,*
>   *A star has fallen;*
> *'Twere better thou shouldst wait until the sunrise.*
> *The fragrance of the new-mown hay*
>   *Arises from the plain.*

FORSAKEN.

More softly the moon looks down on thee, than on others—
Would she tell thee a secret, then,
That she looks more softly down on thee, than on others?

In thy girdle wear a flower,
And make believe to all that thou art happy—
Yea, and look up at heaven, for it alone
   Can understand thy sorrow.
The birds sing songs to thee, but vain is their singing,
They cannot make thee smile,
For thou art she, whom smiles have all forsaken.
Thou dost hear his step, that goeth hence to that other—
And thou know'st his step, as it sounds on that other's
      threshold ;
And the heart of the wife is full of rising tears,
   As the buds are full of sap.
But yet from thee there shall come no blossom forth,
A desert is thy heart, like a grave forsaken ;
Thy heart is like a field where falls no dew,
For the dew of thy tears no more doth touch thy husband,
And his wife's white veil is fair to his eyes no more.
His eyes love that other's veil, that other's smiling ;
And thou art she, whom smiles have all forsaken.

"Mother," the children ask : "why dost smile no longer?"
Then dost thou say to them : " Lo, ye are his children!"
And weepest sore, and his house with thy tears is darkened,
    As the mist doth darken the plains.
Then thy husband flees from the house, because it is
      darkened,
And saith to that other : " Behold, my house is darkened."
And when thou seest her, then dost thou start and tremble,
As though thou didst love her, whom thou durst not hate ;
For ye twain have the self-same love.
Her sin, that begets thy sorrow, thou sorely hatest,
    Yet dost envy her her sin,
For heavier weighs on thee thy sinless sorrow,
    Far heavier, than sin. ·
And thou dost grieve that thou hast no curse upon thee,
That thou canst not say : " I suffer through the curse."
And thy children thou dost not love, for they are his
      children,
Yet lovest them all the more, that they are his children ;
Thou dost hear his step, that goeth hence to that other,
And knowest that he helps her draw the water
Up from the well, and loves the path she hath trodden,
The while he shuns the path that thou didst take.
For his wife's white veil is fair to his eyes no longer.

More softly the moon looketh down on thee than on others ;
Would she tell thee a secret, then,
That she looks more softly down on thee than on others?

HE WHO REMEMBERS.

The cow has fall'n—the little cow-herd weeps.
The rain has washed the pebbles upon the way.
Black flowers have I upon my mantle white.

I SAID to him who remembers,
"What is it that thou dost see?"
He answered: "I see my heart."
Then I said to him: "Look at the mountains,
Look at the plains, and the mill
That waits to rest till the sunset,
And waits till the sunrise to waken;
Then look at the houses, their pitchers
All brimming over with water,
And everywhere mats on the ground,
And daggers upon the wall.
Or see the fountain, that boweth
And raiseth itself again,
Like the forest when wind is blowing;
The streets, where behind their waggons,
The men call aloud as they go.
Oh, do but look at it all!"
"I see only my heart," he answered,
"And it is so dark therein

That I scarce can tell what it holdeth,
But if I turn for a moment
Mine eyes away, there is Something
Moveth within, and that Something
Saith to me : Look at thy heart."

The cow has fall'n—the little cow-herd weeps.
The rain hath washed the pebbles upon the roads,
Black flowers have I upon my mantle white.

THE COBZAR'S LAST SONG.

THE merry Spring, he is my brother,
    And when he comes this way
Each year again, he always asks me:
    "Art thou not yet grown grey?"
But I, I keep my youth for ever,
    Even as the Spring his May.

To ride and hunt the whole world over
    I want no flying steed,
For I have seen it all, each village,
    And every flowery mead;
Men's hearts and their desires, though never
    They showed them me, indeed!

No cloud I need be, through the heavens
    From end to end to fly—
For just as though it were my dwelling,
    I know the broad blue sky;
And thus I say to all the people:
    "My house is there on high."

H

And once, indeed, a little maiden
　　Would give her heart to me,
Her tender heart, but I made answer:
　　"Thus do I counsel thee,
O maiden, keep it for some other,
　　Mine it may never be!"

As onward through the whispering forest
　　Upon my way I sped:
"Whence didst thou get, I prithee tell me,
　　Thy songs?" the forest said.
"From each one of thy leaves," I answered,
　　"Thy green leaves over head."

Upon the luteplayer's grave red flowers
　　In freshest bloom shall keep,
The sun will love to look upon them,
　　And even be fain to creep
Down to the grave where lies the Cobzar,
　　To see him in his sleep.

There with his songs the Cobzar lieth,
　　Nor feeleth lonely so;
And Earth will thank him for his singing
　　Who did her beauty know,
And sang of it—her springs and winters,
　　Her joys, her hopes, her woe.

Then will the luteplayer awaken
  With joyful heart and young,
Because his songs, amid the living,
  Are still on every tongue;
And tales of his, by children's cradles,
  To lull the babes are sung.

"Where is my lute?" he will be asking,
  When he awakes once more;
"My mantle, that was wont to cover
  My heart so well before?
Where is my heart, indeed, that treasured
  So many songs of yore?"

And when the grave to him remembrance
  Of that his death doth bring,
Then will he smile, as dead he lieth,
  O'er that and everything;
And turn him with a smile to slumber
  Again, remembering.

As for his songs—a dewy blossom
  Shall spring from every one,
The dew men drink for hearts' refreshing;
  His grave beneath the sun
Will be so green, that all the weary
  Shall sit them down thereon.

And all shall take him for their brother,
  Who wept with them and smiled ;
And Mother Earth shall claim him, saying :
  " Behold, this was my child."
The luteplayer's grave, the sun doth love it ;
  And shines thereon so mild. '

The merry Spring, he is my brother,
  And when he comes this way
Each year again, he always asks me :
  " Art thou not yet grown grey ? "
But I, I keep my youth for ever,
  Even as the Spring his May.

SPINNING SONGS.

SPINNING SONGS.[1]

I.

The child was weary, it has gone to sleep.

COME down to-morrow to the river-side,
We will pluck flowers together,
The white ones thou, and I the crimson ones;
And thou shalt put the white ones in thy hair,
The crimson I will cast upon the road,
That they may wither 'neath the wand'rer's step.
   —Oh, sister,
Why hast thou no compassion for the flowers?—

The child was weary, it has gone to sleep.

Into the maize-field come with me to-morrow,
There we shall see the sun, and then the moon;
The sun will be for thee, for me the moon.
And thou shalt bless the sun,
But I the moon shall curse.—
     Oh, sister,
Why hast thou no compassion for the moon?—

The child was weary, it has gone to sleep.

[1] Note 5.

Come to draw water from the well to-morrow,
There will we fill our pitchers ;
And thou shalt drink from one till it is empty ;
The other I will break.—
    Oh, sister,
Why hast no pity for the crystal water ?—

    The child was weary, it has gone to sleep.

Shalt come with me to-morrow to the fields ;—
There we shall find two lads,
One very sad, the other one right merry.
Thine is the merry one, and mine the sad.
Thou on the lips wilt kiss the merry one.
The sad one I shall slay.—
    Oh, sister,
Why hast thou no compassion for his sadness ?

    The child was weary, it has gone to sleep.

II.

Oʜ, look no more on me, I have grown old.

—And thou dost yearn for youth.
Then dost thou come and stand upon thy threshold
That thou the yearning mayst forget;
But it forgets thee not—and follows thee,
Speaking with voice as of a little child:
And lo! thou seest thyself as once thou wert,
When very young thou wert—
Three flowers in thy girdle,
Two flowers behind thine ear.—

Oh, look no more on me, I have grown old.—

Yet will I look, for I would see thy pain.
The plain is budding, through it flows the river;
Why dost not sit thee down beside the river,
And beg of it to bear thy pain away,
Away from thee, far out into the world,
That thou mayst hear no talk of it again?—

Oh, look no more on me, I have grown old.

Let be my pain,
For it belongeth to the house ;
What would the house do without pain, I wonder ?
It brings me Night—and every day it brings
Three flowers for my girdle,
Two flowers for mine ear.
In vain I say to it : "Why, dost not see
How old I am, and have no use for flowers ? "
Beside the window I lie down and watch
The dawning of the day.
And the day wonders at the world's fair splendour.
Time was, the day did wonder at my beauty,
　　When I was young.

　　Oh, look no more on me, I have grown old.

III.

I had two flowers. One is withered now ;
The other mourneth for her sister.

WHY dost thou tremble, neighbour ?—

—I saw One pass—
No wanderer it was.—

Who was it then, that thou art trembling thus ?—

—It was the child, the child
That I yet bear within me,
That from my womb escaped,
To look upon the world before its birth.—

—Neighbour ! Thou didst but dream it.—

I had two flowers. One is withered now ;
The other mourneth for her sister.

Now will the child be sad, here in my womb,
For it has seen the earth ;

And seen that I am wan with bearing it ;
Yea, seen that Earth is reeking with man's sweat,
And that she covereth the dust of man.—

—All this it will forget, oh, neighbour, neighbour !
When once it sees the sun.

I had two flowers.   One is withered now ;
The other mourneth for her sister.

IV.

Be silent! for my sister slumbereth,
  And if she be awakened, then she weeps.—

—I will not wake her, have no fear; but this,
This only, I must tell thee:
'Twas at the season of the linden's flowering,
'Twas then she died. And they did take her from me,
Leaving me naught of her, except her necklet,
The necklet from her throat,
That once was warmed all through by her warm blood.
Upon a nail I hung it, on the wall
And put a spray of basil over it.
The little necklace never moves, and yet
  The beads all talk together,
Whene'er the sun peeps in and makes them glitter;
Then do they look like tears upon the wall.
And when the sun comes in, one sees full well
That withered is the spray of basil now.—

Be silent! for my sister slumbereth,
  And if she be awakened, then she weeps.—

I will not wake her, but just this alone—
I must yet tell thee, that the beads all say :
" Why do they leave us hanging on the wall—
Beside this withered branch ?
The whole day long do we await the sun,
And when he comes, he makes us look like tears.
The tears run down, and then the tears dry up,
But we remain for ever."
She died, and they have taken her away,
  Away from me, and left me naught of her,
      Except this necklet.—

Be silent ! for my sister slumbereth,
  And if she be awakened, then she weeps.

V.

The fire is slumb'ring,
Who will waken it?

He whom I love spake thus to me:
  "Give me thy songs;"
So I have given him all my songs,
And now he sings them, that he may be strong
About his work—for in those songs I told him
That sunshine says to Earth:
"Thou shalt bear most beauteous children,
  If so be thy sons are brave."

The fire is slumb'ring,
Who will waken it?

He whom I love spake thus to me:
  "Tell me thy dreams;"
So then I told him all my dreams,
  And he remembers them;
  For in my dreams I saw
A Heiduck proud, his right hand red with blood.

And thus, I told him, sunshine speaks to Earth :
  " Brave children thou wilt have,
If on their hands thy men bear stains of blood."

> *The fire is slumb'ring,*
> *Who will waken it ?*

He whom I love, spake thus to me :
" Tell me, how thou wilt sleep within the Earth ? "—
So then I told, and hearing, he was glad ;
For I shall sleep, down there within the Earth,
With open eyes, and on my face a smile ;
And in my eyes the Earth will be,
  And in my mouth.
I told him that the sunshine says to Earth :
  " Brave children thou wilt have
If they but understand how they may sleep
  Right well in thee."

> *The fire is slumb'ring,*
> *Who will waken it ?*

VI.

My girdle I hung on a tree-top tall,
So the songs of the birds, it bears them all.

O MAIDEN, who gave thee those lips so red,
That smile, and those songs ?—
              —Lad, what is it to thee
Or why wouldst thou know who hath given them me—
—And whither, O maiden, so fast art thou sped ?
To the plum-tree groves in the valley below,
  Or there, where the orchards of apple-trees grow
Overhanging the cliff ?—
             —Lad, what is it to thee,
Since it is not thou that shalt go with me ?—

My girdle I hung on a tree-top tall,
So the songs of the birds, it bears them all.

O maiden, and what in thy heart dost thou bear ?
A song, or a love ?—
             —Lad, what is it to thee ?
If there's one that I love, sure, thou art not he.—
Where wouldst thou I died of my love, then, where ?

I

By the river, where over me flowers shall weep?
In the hut, where the mother who lulled me to sleep,
Shall sing me my dirge?—
                                    —Lad, what is it to me,
Since I am not going to weep over thee?—

My girdle I hung on a tree-top tall,
  So the songs of the birds, it hears them all.

VII.

He turned his head, he turned his head away,
But whether he was glad, I do not know.

WHY hast thou, brother, no compassion on her?
Weary she is, remorseful, and alone.—
—And didst thou go within her house, my sister?
What saw'st thou in the house?—
—I saw the little house was very poor;
No flowers in the window,
No mat upon the threshold;
Hard as the heart of the wicked was her bed,
I said: "Thou wouldst lie softer on bare earth."—

He turned his head, he turned his head away,
But whether he was glad, I do not know.

What didst thou see, my sister, in the courtyard?—
—Naught save some hay, all blackened by the rain,
And then a dried-up well,
    Dry as a widow's heart.—
—What didst thou see upon her face, my sister?—
—Furrows I saw upon her face, like ruts

Upon the roads when they are full of rain ;
    And full of tears were these.

He turned his head, he turned his head away,
But whether he was glad, I do not know.

Hast thou no pity on her, brother, brother ?—
—The carrion hath no pity on the vulture
That dies for having rent it and devoured it.

He turned his head, he turned his head away,
But whether he was glad, I do not know.

VIII.

What dost thou bear in thine apron, little heart ?

FLOWERS I bear, and grass, and fruit from the garden.
My little mother died in the spring at even,
And I think of her, since then, in the long spring evenings,
Then do I hear no more the mill-wheel's murmur.
I put on my bravest dress
When I go to see my mother, there in the graveyard,
That so I may seem right merry to my mother.
And when I have the year's first-fruits, I fail not
To cast across my threshold two of them,
Yea, twain I give to the road, I give to the wand'rer,
That in Earth's depths my mother may not hunger.

What dost thou bear in thine apron, little heart ?

The stranger came and said: "Why goest not with me?
My village stands beside a cool, green valley,
Where flights of birds come by, and even in flying
They tarry on my cottage."
Then to the stranger I spake thus: "O stranger,
Go home without me, I would tarry here;

The sun and moon are wont to see me always
Here in my little hut;
And a strange house would have no room, O stranger,
For these my sorrows and my joys; no corner
Would there be found for me to stand my distaff,
And ever would thy house be saying, stranger,
" Of joys and sorrows we've enough already,
      We have no room for thine ! "

What dost thou bear in thine apron, little heart?

IX.

Oh, stay beside me, for alone am I.

O MOTHER, when my hair has all grown white
I'll shroud my veil so close about my head
That none will see my hair has grown so white ;
And I shall know so many, many things ;
 Shall know, why thou dost weep.
And he I love, he too will then be old,
Will put his cap of fur upon his head,
That none may see how white his hair has grown ;
And I can say, at last, I love him, then.
So often shall I tell him so,
That it will make him grow quite young again.
And I shall say to him : " Dost thou remember
Upon that day, beside the well, when I
 Would never smile on thee ?
 That was because I loved thee."
Mother, but I would fain be growing old
That I might tell him sooner !

Oh, stay beside me, for alone am I.

And the young maidens then will beg of me
To tell them of my life—and I will tell them
About my life and all its many joys.—

The tree doth think no more, my little daughter,
About its fruit, when winter-time has come;
And thou, thou too, thy smiles wilt all forget.

O mother, O dear mother, say not so!
Because I smile with twofold joy, to think
I shall remember them when I am sad,
    Too sad, to smile again.—
—My child, the birds do carol every spring,
    Yet not the self-same birds.
The harvests ripen every year, but yet
Each time new seeds are sown.
Even so the heart of man sings once, once only;
Once, and once only, doth his harvest ripen.—

—O mother, O dear mother, say not so!
For when I have grown old
I'll smile upon the birds and on the harvests,
And say to them, "I too once bloomed and sang."

Oh, stay beside me, for alone am I.

X.

Tell me who she is, oh, tell me!—

—SHE hath no mother more, and her father's name
    Is all unknown to me.
With her, the self-same moment, flowers were born—
    With her the flowers will die.
Nay, nay, I love her not; yet I look at her.
She wanders through the forest, and thereat
    The forest doth rejoice.—

    —Tell me who she is, oh, tell me!—

—If Death should take
That which is sweetest upon earth away,
    He would take her.
Strong will the children be that are born of her,
And from her breast the milk will stream in plenty,
Like rivers at the melting of the snow.—

    Tell me who she is, oh, tell me!

XI.

Go draw me water from the well,
I am athirst.—

AH ! what and if the well were dry ?—
—Then there is yet the river.—
—What if the river were dried up ?—
—Then hath the spring still water ;
But oh ! a joyless heart, that hath
    No other joy beside.—
—What hath befallen this thy heart ?—
—They came and took its joy away,
They came by night to take its joy,
And all the way was dark.

   Go draw me water from the well,
    I am athirst.

And if the swallow were to die,
Yet were the lark still here ;
And if the hail laid low our corn,
The hay were left us still ;
But oh ! a loveless life, that hath
    No other love beside.—

—What hath befallen that thy love?—
—My love is dead. They murdered it
    With a sure knife and sharp,
And with a hand that trembled not ;
    I saw its blood,
Its blood, that through my fingers flowed ;
I could not stay the stream.

  Go draw me water from the well,
    I am athirst.

XII.

Which dost thou love to hear the best,
My spindle or my voice?—

THREE lads have died in the village there,
And one was my belovèd.
Water from out the stream he drank,
There, where a star had bathed,
And then he died; and I bewail him,
And sing my songs o'er him.
I see the star in the water still,
But he shall see it no more.

Which dost thou love to hear the best,
My spindle or my voice?

I said to the star: "For two whole nights
I would gaze on naught save thee,
If thou wouldst tell me where bides his soul.
Is it there in the flowers? in my bracelet here?
Or yon 'mid the ripe red corn?
For if I knew 'twas in a flower,
I would water it oft and tend it well,
That it might bloom for aye.

And if 'twere in my bracelet here,
I'd pillow my head upon mine arm,
That so I might have fairest dreams—
Yea, dreams all robed in white.
And if 'twere in the ripe red corn,
My sickle ne'er should mow it down,
But I would pluck it gently."

> *Which dost thou love to hear the best,*
> *My spindle or my voice ?*

Then thus the star replied to me :
" His soul is so far away,
That though thou shouldst take the fleetest steed,
Thou couldst not reach it ever.
Stay rather, leaning by thy hut,
Perchance the little soul will come,
    Come flying up to thee ;
Yet never seek to hold it there,
But give it straight the fleetest steed,
That it may hasten hence once more,
    That it may haste away."

> *Which dost thou love to hear the best,*
> *My spindle or my voice ?*

XIII.

Upon my threshold thou wilt meet
An agèd man—him shalt thou bid come in.

Do not thou ask that maid again
Whither she fares—she knows it not herself,
But loveth to go wand'ring round about;
And those who pass her by disturb her not.
She wanders thus because she hath all knowledge
Of magic philtres.   One she drank herself,
Not knowing that she drank it, and since then
The world is changed to her, and all the world
To her seems old—yea, thou art aged, and I;
The forest has grown old—an hundred years;
And she herself alone, she thinks, is young.
She laugheth at our age—and wandereth on
Along the ways, to find the youth who'll love her;
But never will she find him.

Before my threshold thou wilt meet
An agèd man—him shalt thou bid come in.

XIV.

Pluck no more flowers before her,
For she never gathers one.

WHITHER the streams are flowing,
O mother, dost thou know ?—
—To the villages, through the forests,
And o'er the plains they wend.—
—And whither tears go streaming,
O mother, dost thou know ?
Tears that are wept by women,
Tears that they wipe away
With the back of their hand, and that trembling
Upon the hand yet lie ?—
—Tears flow into graves, to comfort
The dead for having died.—

Pluck no more flowers before her,
For she never gathers one.

Who was it, this evening, mother,
That thou didst let in to thee ?—
—A woman it was, who sorely
Wept o'er her womb, that bears

Only dead children ever.
She weeps, that the souls of those children
Have never looked on earth,
And she prays the souls of those children
To turn them back for a moment
That she may look on them.—

> *Pluck no more flowers before her,*
> *For she never gathers one.*

And hath she not her cottage
Wherein she may tarry, mother ?—
—Nay, she was fain to show me
Her tears—and they flowed before me ;
And she said of those unknown children :
"Golden hair like the sunrise
One would have had—and that other
Cheeks as red as the sunset ;
Slender, like as my distaff,
She would have grown, and beside me
Singing would she have sat.
Yet dead in my womb I bare them.
Then Nature spake thus to me, saying,
'Art thou a grave ?'"

> *Pluck no more flowers before her,*
> *For she never gathers one.*

NOTES.

NOTE 1.

"THE other women have their veils," is as much as to say "they are married;" for only married women may wear veils on their heads in Roumania.

NOTE 2.

"Thy belt six turns doth make about thy waist." The slenderness of a girl is measured by the number of times she can twist her long soft belt or girdle about her waist.

NOTE 3.

The phrase "sister of the cross" has been used by the translators to denote a sort of elective relationship which is common in Roumania, and is distinguished by the untranslatable word "surata" a mere variation of "sora," a sister. It is usual there for two girls who may be no relation to each other, to choose one other out as sisters, and this choice is hallowed by a special service in church, during which their feet are chained together, to symbolize the bond that is henceforth to unite them. This is regarded as so real a one, that marriage with the brother of one's elective sister is forbidden, nor can these two "sisters" marry two brothers.

NOTE 4.

It is the custom in Roumanian villages to paint a flower on the wall of a house it which a maiden lives; but if she is known to have behaved ill, the village youths come and efface the painting from the wall.

K

NOTE 5.

For the Spinning-songs, the girls all stand in a circle, spinning; the best spinner and singer being in the middle. She begins to improvise a song, and at any moment she chooses, throws her spindle, holding it by a long thread, to another girl, who has to go on spinning while the first girl pulls out the flax—a proceeding requiring great dexterity—and at the same time has to continue the improvisation which has been begun.

CHISWICK PRESS:—CHARLES WHITTINGHAM AND CO., TOOKS COURT, CHANCERY LANE.